A CELEBRATION OF

SELF,
PLAYFULNESS,
AND EXPLORATION

LOOK AT ME

written by Audrey Beth Stein   illustrated by Kristina Neudakhina

Hardcover ISBN: 978-0-578-96531-4
Paperback ISBN: 979-8548608529

I like to wear
nail polish.

Purses and patent leather make me feel glamorous.

I don't want to feel
glamorous.

Suits are boring.

Skirts are cold.

I like suits.

Me too.

My mom makes me
wear frilly dresses.

I hate that.

My parents let us wear whatever we want,
as long as they can buy it on sale.

I'm going to wear my
Monday underwear.

Pajamas make good ears.

Can I wear pigtails today?

I have clown hair.

I like short hair.
Goodbye, pigtails!

Uh-oh.

Will it grow long again
in time for my birthday party?

I like Mommy's clothes.

I like her jewelry,
and Daddy's ties.

One of my mommies
never wears dresses.
My other mommy sometimes
wears dresses.

I *love* dresses.
I hate tights though.

Pants are itchy.
I like tights.

When I grow up, I'm going to wear
everything.

When I grow up, I'm going to live
somewhere warm
and be *naked* all the time.

Wheee!

Look at me!

Lightning Source UK Ltd.
Milton Keynes UK
UKHW050711141221
395614UK00002B/39

"Just another normal day for Team X!" said Max.
"No more dinosaurs today though, please!" laughed Mini.

Now you have read ...
T. rex Trouble

Take a closer look

How many different verbs can you find that tell you how the characters move?

Read these sentences and choose the *best* verb to use each time:

A huge, scaly head _____ through the trees.

popped up	appeared	burst

Max and Mini _____ away from the T. rex.

walked	sped	trotted

Max and Mini _____ across the gully.

flew	went	soared

Thinking time

How did Max and Mini get across the gully? Can you complete the sentence?

Max and Mini_____across the_____ on Max's_____.

24